This book belongs to:

Rainbow Dash

The
WONDERBOLTS
Academy Handbook

Little, Brown and Company

Hachette Book Group
1290 Avenue of the Americas, New York, NY 10104
Visit us at lb-kids.com

Little, Brown and Company is a division of Hachette Book Group, Inc. The Little, Brown name and logo are trademarks of Hachette Book Group, Inc.

The publisher is not responsible for websites (or their content) that are not owned by the publisher.

First Edition: July 2016

ISBN 978-0-316-39499-4

Library of Congress Control Number: 2016937665

10 9 8 7 6 5 4 3 2 1

WOR

Jacket title font set in Generation B by Harold's Fonts
Printed in the United States of America

The
WONDERBOLTS
Academy Handbook

Admiral
Sherbert
Burst

By ~~Brandon T. Snider~~

Little, Brown and Company
New York Boston

UTENTES SUPERIORES
"SOARING HIGHER!"

Dear Cadet,

Congratulations. Your exemplary academic accomplishments and personal achievements are impressive and outstanding. They have allowed you entry into one of the most elite institutions in Equestria. From all of the staff, as well as the current student body—Welcome to the Wonderbolts Academy!

This handbook establishes our Wonderbolts Academy guidelines and the code of conduct for you to follow during your time here. It's been revised over many moons for each new class of cadets. It's important that you read it thoroughly and completely. This book contains priceless information that has

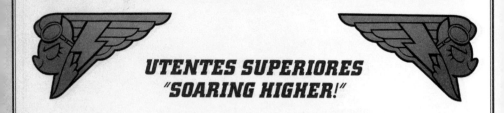

positively influenced ponies for centuries. Treat it with the respect it deserves, and absorb its knowledge to the fullest extent. We want you to feel challenged so you can grow into the best pony you can possibly be. Should you have any questions about the information contained within these pages, feel free to approach any member of our faculty. They will be happy to help clarify its many lessons and teachings. Remember: You're surrounded by friends.

Good luck on your journey. We're very excited that you're here!

See you in the clouds,

Headmaster Wing

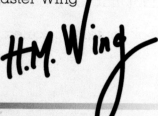

CONTENTS

THE LEGEND OF THE WONDERBOLTS

"Mares and gentlecolts and foals of all ages, look to the skies and prepare to be awestruck by the incredible flying prowess of the Wonderbolts!"

After Princess Luna was banished to the moon, Princess Celestia knew she needed to build a coalition of Earth ponies, Unicorns, and Pegasi to help safeguard Equestria's future from harm's way. She soon drafted a handful of brave ponies

1

to become the E.U.P. Guard of Protective Pony Platoons. This elite peacekeeping force served Equestria quite well. Princess Celestia was greatly impressed with their commitment and dedication. When the celebration of Equestria's first Celestial Year of Peace began, General Firefly selected seven top Pegasi from the E.U.P. to perform a series of death-defying aerial stunts. These expert flyers dazzled the crowd with their twists, turns, and stunning group formations. It was clear that these ponies knew what true teamwork and commitment were all about. Their amazing performance stunned the audience as magical lightning filled the sky! General Firefly saw the potential for greatness in this impressive squad of ponies. He believed there was great talent within them that was worth nurturing; all it would take was patience and guidance. General Firefly dubbed these high-flying daredevils the Wonderbolts and dedicated his career to shaping their future. His mission was to build a group of noble, dignified ponies who exhibited all the positive qualities that good leaders possess. A Wonderbolt would know the value of teamwork and how to support their fellow teammates. A Wonderbolt would always be true to themselves and learn how to stay disciplined under pressure. It was a lofty goal but one that he knew he could achieve.

Soon word got out, and Equestria was buzzing far and wide about General Firefly's amazing and exclusive battalion. *Everypony* wanted to be a Wonderbolt. The time finally came when General Firefly knew he had to think even bigger. He had to have true vision if the Wonderbolts were ever going to reach new heights. Then one day, while soaring high above the clouds, an idea came to him. He would start a school, a place where ponies would learn amazing aerial feats. Not only that, they'd also develop personal responsibility and the basic tools to help them excel at being the best

ponies they could
possibly be. Soon
the Wonderbolts
Academy was
born, and thus
began a legendary
institution for
the ages. Many
famous cadets
have passed
through the halls
of the Academy
since its humble
beginnings.
But a cadet
doesn't need

to become famous in order to succeed. General
Firefly believed that every young cadet who trots
through the doors of the Wonderbolts Academy
has something great to offer. With training and
diligence, a Wonderbolt can SOAR!

MANY PONIES, ONE EQUESTRIA

ALICORNS

have a Unicorn horn, Pegasus wings, and sometimes an Earth pony power. They are very rare and rule throughout Equestria.

PEGASI

use their wings to fly, walk among the clouds, and control the weather.

EARTH PONIES
have a unique connection to nature, animals, and plants.

UNICORNS
have a special horn that allows them to perform magic.

THE WONDERBOLTS ACADEMY CAMPUS RULES FOR SCHOOL

The Wonderbolts Academy is the birthplace of aviation and a beacon of excellence known throughout Equestria. It's where a bright, young pony can get the education they need in order to excel in all aspects of ponyhood. The engaging campus keeps cadets occupied day and night. They should familiarize themselves with its many iconic structures. Behold the wonder!

WONDERBOLTS HEADQUARTERS

During your stay at the Wonderbolts Academy, treat it as your second home and respect your surroundings. Cadets caught littering and causing mayhem will be punished accordingly.

THE LANDING STRIP

Always stay cautious and aware near the Landing Strip area, looking both ways before crossing the runway. Most accidents can be prevented by using common sense.

THE BARRACKS

Living with other ponies can be challenging, especially when you're on top of one another in a tight space. Communal living at the Wonderbolts Academy is about getting to know your fellow cadets. Strike up a conversation during mealtime or while you're cooking breakfast. If you see a cadet struggling with something, take the time to help them out. Things won't always be bright and easy, but set realistic expectations for your experience. Know that there will be some days when you'll want to be surrounded by a supportive network of friends, and other days when you'll feel like being alone. That's okay! Take everything one step at a time.

FUN FACT

Admiral Fairweather built the Barracks area completely by hoof.

SLEEPING QUARTERS

Keep your conversations at a low level when in the Sleeping Quarters. Respect those cadets who use their downtime to rest and recharge.

REMEMBER: NO HORSING AROUND AFTER HOURS WILL BE TOLERATED.

FUN FACT

The cadet with the slowest times from the day's drills is typically charged with cleaning the compound.

LOCKER ROOMS

Keeping the Locker Rooms clean is of the utmost importance. Turn off all faucets and remove all used towels from the premises after showering. No lingering.

CLASSROOMS

Employ basic etiquette when in a classroom setting. Raise your hoof if you have a question or need to use the restroom. Respect your fellow cadets by letting them speak and be heard. No one likes a rude pony.

LIBRARY

The Library is the perfect place for a cadet to study quietly without being disturbed. Use the expansive chamber to read up on a topic you're curious about or investigate a subject for an essay you're writing. Seminars on basic and efficient study skills are available on a quarterly basis and are first come, first serve.

COMMON AREAS

Socializing is encouraged at the Wonderbolts Academy! Utilize the common areas to play an assortment of team-building activities or to lounge around and unwind.

MEMORABILIA DISPLAY CASE

You can feel the history of the Wonderbolts Academy throughout every inch of the campus. Keeping the past close-at-hoof is a reminder of how much progress has been made since the Wonderbolts first appeared. Notable Wonderbolts memorabilia on display within the Barracks

include General Flash's famous cap and the original team crest. Let yesteryear inspire new generations to greatness. There's always work to be done!

EXPLORE CLOUDSDALE

The Wonderbolts Academy is nestled in a place that has been called "the greatest city in the sky" by *Equestria Magazine*. Welcome to the enchanted world of Cloudsdale! A cadet should get to know their surroundings, especially when they're in unfamiliar territory. Learn about history and customs by visiting local monuments and patronizing businesses. Being in a new location is an opportunity to experience unique cultures. Step outside of your comfort zone and get to know Cloudsdale up close.

WEATHER FACTORY

Where is weather made? The Weather Factory of course! Take a group tour or apply for an internship to learn about Cloudsdale's most famous export. Classes in Weather Making are available on weekends and cover the atmosphere, how a rainbow gets made, how snowflakes form, and where rain comes from.

CLOUDOSSEUM

The Cloudosseum plays host to exciting and important events such as the Wonderbolts Derby and the Equestria Games. Cadets receive discounted tickets to all events at the Cloudosseum and are encouraged to attend.

FUN FACT

Transportation from Equestria below is provided daily for visitors via hot-air balloon!

LESSON #1

BALANCE & DISCIPLINE

Attending the Wonderbolts Academy means taking on a considerable workload. Cadets must attend class, organize study sessions, and train on a daily basis. It can be *a lot* to take on for a young pony. And how does that leave any time for fun? This is where balance and discipline are needed. **BALANCE** is learning to manage studies, schooling, and personal time without overcommitting to too many activities. DISCIPLINE is sticking to a set schedule and giving yourself just the right amount of time to enjoy the things you like while still getting your work done. Making

a plan to follow a daily regimen is the first step on the path to success!

Begin your plan the night before you intend to start your regimen. Start by making a list of all the things you need to accomplish the next day, beginning in the morning and ending in the evening. The following day, check off tasks as you complete them and, at the end of the day, take stock of what you've accomplished. Make sure to note any impromptu activities you engage in. Do this for a week and, at the end of the experience, look over each day's itinerary. What did you spend the most time doing? Are you spending too much time having fun and not enough committing to your studies? Are you taking too many classes, leaving you no time for your friends? There are always ways to reposition your schooling and personal life so that you can enjoy them both.

REMEMBER:
BALANCE is the best way to ensure harmony!

MEET THE WONDERBOLTS

ACADEMY STAFF

★ A GUIDING FORCE ★

The instructors at the Wonderbolts Academy were once young cadets, just like you. Now they work hard to make sure the next generation gets the best education in the sky. Trust in their expertise and judgment, and communicate with them when you need a helping hoof. That's what they're there for!

MAKING SURE EVERYPONY AT THE ACADEMY KNOWS WHERE TO BE AND WHEN IS A BIG JOB.

Tight Ship is in charge scheduling and knows the value of maintaing a schedule. Showing up on time and getting things done go hoof in hoof. He knows when Wonderbolts are supposed to be *training*, and he knows when Wonderbolts are supposed to be *performing*. Once the day's itinerary is settled on, Tight Ship sticks to it. That's how he keeps things moving in the right direction.

Crescent Moon keeps an eye on things at the Wonderbolts Academy as the school caretaker. With so many students, it can be difficult to manage, but Crescent Moon knows everypony by name and makes himself available whenever they need his council. There's lots of activity on campus and things can fall through the cracks sometimes, but with CM watching, everypony who walks through that front gate is in good hooves.

We all rely on *Fast Clip* to make sure training days run smoothly and efficiently. As a drill instructor, he doesn't waste *any* time getting down to business. It's all about training hard and staying in line. There's zero time for horseplay when Fast Clip is running the show.

Whiplash is one of the toughest instructors at the Academy. He tests ponies *backward* and *forward*, so they better know their stuff! He grades hard, too. There's no extra credit in Whiplash's world. Despite being a pony of  few words, his image as a hoof-buster is mostly a legend. When he isn't putting cadets in their places, he's just a big softie.

★ WHAT IS DOWNTIME? ★

DOWNTIME is for spending time with friends and doing activities that you enjoy. This helps you relax and forget about the stressfulness of the day. Building downtime into your schedule is very important. An overloaded cadet with no time to breathe can be a recipe for trouble. Downtime is about clearing your head and recalibrating. Exercise or games with friends are great ways to relax and alleviate the pressures of the day.

DATA DRILL

★ **WHAT IS BALANCE?**

★ **WHY IS IT IMPORTANT?**

Because who wants to feel
loco in the coco all the time?

★ **DO I NEED TO WORK ON BALANCING
MY TRAINING WITH RELAXATION?
DO I FIND IT DIFFICULT? WHY?**

ALERT! ALERT!
This section is a snooze!

LESSON #2

AUTHORITY & COMMAND

Following the structure of command at the Wonderbolts Academy is essential to a cadet's success. A hierarchy of leadership is a staple of any historic institution and such a framework gives ponies a chance to learn from experienced trailblazers who've served with honor and dignity. Cadets and new recruits would do well to spend time with elder ponies who've served proudly. They've got some great stories! They've also seen and done a lot during their service and deserve to be revered for their expertise and knowledge.

Ponies in positions of power are known as authority figures.

AUTHORITY is the ability to give orders to somepony in a lower position. Authority figures at the Wonderbolts Academy include captains, teachers, and the Wonderbolts themselves. These ponies hold experience, knowledge, and discipline from which younger generations can benefit. Authority figures are knowledgeable in many respects. They understand the importance of study, practice, and development. They were once young and inexperienced themselves, after all! Always listen to authority figures, and let them share the wisdom they've accumulated over time. If you've got a question, don't be afraid to ask. And always make sure you're respectful. Authority figures are who they are because they've earned it!

E.U.P. GUARD OF PROTECTIVE
★ PONY PLATOONS ★

The original Wonderbolts were created from members of the original E.U.P. Guard of Protective Pony Platoons. Through the centuries, this group of courageous and devoted ponies have acted as soldiers, ceremonial guardians, and royal bodyguards. Historically, the E.U.P.'s primary directive has been to protect and serve in a peaceful capacity, with members holding a variety of titles and ranks, but it has evolved over the moons.

★ WHAT IS RANK? ★

A **RANK** is a position within an organization or team. There are different types of ranks for different types of team structures. Rank is based on a variety of factors.

A **LEADER** is a pony with a high rank. A high rank has authority and control over a team's structure and function. A leader has a great deal of applicable experience and is knowledgeable on an assortment of relevant subjects.

A **TEAM MEMBER** is a pony with a mid-level rank. This rank is a very vital part of a team structure. They have completed their education and are directly applying their studies in the field. Team members can become leaders after years of practical experience.

That's me!
-Cadet
Rainbow Dash!

A **CADET** is a pony with a low rank. A cadet is still involved in the training process and must defer to higher-ranking ponies with more experience and schooling.

★ HISTORY'S HEROES ★

It's critical for younger generations to acknowledge and understand the sacrifices of those who came before them. The E.U.P. once comprised a great many leaders who shaped the path of ponies far and wide. Their contributions to Wonderbolts history are unparalleled, and they deserve our esteem and admiration.

With a feisty spirit and a passion for flying, *General Firefly* assembled the original Wonderbolts team from the finest aviators in Equestria. A **GENERAL** is senior command position reserved for decorated veterans who have served proudly.

No other pony commanded adoration like *General Flash*. As the tenth leader of the Wonderbolts, Flash was a decorated leader many times over. He was also a quick thinker.

Commander Easyglider established the classic Wonderbolts choreography with such famous moves as the Chevron Formation, the Icaranian Sun Salutation, and the memorable Sonic Rainboom. Her hard-working style inspired newer

Wonderbolts formations such as the Ringlet, the Chocolate Swirl, and the Mare-Do-Well. A COMMANDER is a high-ranking senior officer who has led an elite squadron of ponies and served with distinction.

As the leader of the Wonderbolts in the Fourth Celestial Era, *Colonel Purple Dart* was known to be full of heart. He always had his friend's backs and never once left pony behind. A **COLONEL** is a high-ranking field officer who is responsible for commanding lower-ranking ponies.

The legendary *Admiral Fairweather* was admired for not only being tough but also unafraid to put his hoof down. When it came to protecting his pony brothers and sisters, Fairweather never backed down from a bully. An **ADMIRAL** is a high-ranking officer who oversees the day-to-day operations of a pony platoon.

Admiral Fairy Flight led the 7th Squadron of Wonderbolts and had a style all her own. Her spunky demeanor and positive outlook still serves as an inspiration to foals of all ages.

QUESTION:

Why do I have to learn about all of these old ponies?

ANSWER:

Well, Rainbow Dash, history is **EVERYWHERE** and without the groundbreaking ponies of the past, I might not even be here!

TIPS FOR TRIUMPH

ALWAYS address a higher-ranking officer
by their full rank title.

DATA DRILL

★ **WHO HAS AUTHORITY AT WONDERBOLTS ACADEMY?**

Teachers, generals, leaders, commanders, ponies who are wearing lots of medals, ponies who sit at desks with lots of papers on them, the pony who cleans the mess hall after lunch?

★ **DO I HAVE AUTHORITY?**

★ **HOW DOES MY RANK AFFECT MY ABILITY TO GIVE ORDERS?**

★ **IS IT EVER OKAY TO GIVE ORDERS TO A TEAM MEMBER?**

YEAH!

LESSON #3

LEADERSHIP

At the Wonderbolts Academy, we believe
that all of our cadets have the ability to become
fantastic leaders who'll rise to the challenges
of the future. A pony can be a leader in many
different ways and in many different places.
LEADERSHIP isn't about being in charge; it's about
setting a positive example that will inspire others
to do great things. A cadet can practice leadership
in all aspects of their day-to-day life by helping
out at home, being attentive in their studies, and
playing an active role in the community.

✶ *HOW TO BE A LEADER* ✶

Surround yourself with encouraging influences and avoid negativity.

Learn how to spot bullying and stand up to bullies when you see them behaving badly and demeaning their fellow cadets.

Keep an open mind and do your best to understand where your fellow cadets are coming from. Put yourself in another pony's hooves, and you may learn about yourself in the process.

Embolden younger ponies to follow a path of leadership and set good examples for them to follow. Future generations need guidance from positive role models.

⚡

Be honest and forthright with yourself and others. Always look for a gracious way to tell the truth.

⚡

Everypony goes through tough times. When you see a cadet struggling and in need, help them. Be a friend and let them know they aren't alone.

★ *LEARNING TO FAIL* ★

When a cadet fails, it doesn't mean they give up. Remember, failure is part of life. It helps you grow and learn, so the next time you encounter failure, you know how to handle it. Leaders know that they won't always excel at every single thing they attempt to do, but it doesn't mean they stop trying. It's okay to be disappointed. *Every* leader has failed before. What's meaningful is that you learn to accept the loss and move forward. Nopony ever succeeded by focusing on the negative. If you're having trouble letting go, don't be afraid to ask your fellow cadet for advice. You're never alone at the Wonderbolts Academy!

✦ COMPROMISE ✦

Sometimes it can be difficult to make everypony happy. Leadership requires the ability to listen to many different opinions and make an informed decision on the topic at hand. There may be instances where a particular decision makes some cadets experience positive results and other cadets experience negative results. This can often be avoided by negotiating a compromise to the situation. A COMPROMISE involves listening to all perspectives and coming up with a balanced solution. Compromises can be hard-won for some cadets because it requires giving up something that they may have wanted. In the end, however, compromise is a much better solution than abandoning a decision all together.

MENTORSHIP &
★ ENCOURAGEMENT ★

When a good leader sees a struggling cadet, they will always take them under their wing. Being a mentor to a budding young flyer helps them to see a clearer path to success. Share with them the things you've learned that have helped you grow. Tell them some of the mistakes you've made so they don't fall into a negative pattern. Encourage them to keep going in a positive direction.

Attaining Wonderbolt status takes patience and dedication. The road isn't always easy, but with optimistic peers and internal fortitude, a committed cadet can achieve great things!

GET TO KNOW
✦ YOUR FELLOW PONIES ✦

While your fellow cadets are all Pegasi, they, along with Earth ponies and Unicorns, are all a part of the pony community, and each group has something very special to offer one another. A leader takes the time to get to know the diversity of ponies that surround them. Share your experiences, your hopes for the future, and even the things that might scare you. Use your free time to play games and engage in bonding activities. This will build a sense of comradeship and strengthen bonds of ponyhood that will last a lifetime.

✦ *MAKING DECISIONS* ✦

Leaders are constantly facing challenging choices. There's a lot of information out there to consider when you're faced with a tough decision. A leader always considers the pros and cons of the situation. A **PRO** is a factor that can result in a positive outcome, and a **CON** is a factor that can result in a negative outcome. Thinking about the good and bad outcomes will help a cadet make better choices.

EXAMPLE

CADET #1:

Let's skip class today and go practice flying!
We'll say "too sick" to go to attend. *Shhhh.*
Don't tell anypony what we're up to.

CADET #2:

Hmmmm. I'm not sure about this...

PRO

PRO #1—Practice is very important to development.

PRO #2—Flying can be fun.

CON

CON #1—Skipping class will cause this cadet to miss crucial information, which will make her fall behind in her studies.

CON #2—Lying about illness and keeping secrets can be very harmful to your friendships as well as your well-being.

QUESTION: Based on these **PROS** and **CONS**, which is a better course of action?

★ *GROUP LEADERSHIP* ★

Group leaders are chosen based on the trust
of their peers and the ability to resolve conflicts
among them. They should also be intelligent and
unafraid to share their thoughtful viewpoints.
If they're funny and have a good personality,
even better! Group leaders service the goals of
the platoon in measurable and positive ways.
A leader should always have a vision, but if a
leader's vision overshadows a group, the leader
can become self-serving. In a case like that, make
sure you speak up. Use your voice when issues
arise. Be mindful of a leader's role and express
your viewpoint decorously. Don't adopt a gang
mentality; it'll just make the situation worse.
Find positive ways to voice your concerns. Group
leaders should also pay attention to developing
conflicts within a group and catch them before they

grow unmanageable. Assuming team members will sort their problems out on their own isn't always a feasible solution. A leader should play an active role in problem solving and troubleshooting concerns as they appear. Leaders will come and go over time. That's part of ponyhood! Embracing new leadership with an open mind is key to maintaining a platoon together. Trust that there is a reason for a leader's selection, and work to correct any misunderstandings that may arise during a change of command.

QUALITIES A LEADER SHOULD POSSESS

The ability to listen to team members

⚡

Sensitivity to team members' concerns

⚡

Problem-solving skills

MEET THE

WONDERBOLTS

SPITFIRE

MY HEROES!

TEAM CAPTAIN, ACADEMY DRILL INSTRUCTOR

As Captain of the Wonderbolts, it's my job to keep my team in line and make sure they know what they're doing. It's not all about loop-de-loops and having fun when you're flying high. You've got to keep your mane in the game. That's why I train my students hard. Every little mare that comes my way is going to learn things the Spitfire way. No free flies. Competition is a great way to keep a Pegasus on their toes, but teamwork is essential when you're zooming through a

through a patch of thick clouds. I'm a drill instructor: I'm not here to be your best friend. Some ponies are intimidated by my methods. They think I've got a temper. To them I say, **YOU ARE WRONG!** But my door is always open.

SPITFIRE

SOARIN

COMMANDER, WONDERBOLTS

It takes lots of hard work to become a Wonderbolt, but it's all worth it in the end. There isn't a feeling in the world like gliding through the air as fast as you can. It's actually kind of relaxing! I think the best thing about being a Wonderbolt is that my teammates always have one another's backs. We've all got secret nicknames, but I'll never tell anypony what they are. You've got to be a

Wonderbolt to find out. After a long
day of flying, I like to treat my 'Bolt
buddies and myself to some nice
apple pie. But mostly I like to treat
myself because **PIE IS THE BEST**.

Soarin

TIPS FOR TRIUMPH

A leader uses a positive and encouraging tone
to guide their fellow pony to greatness.

DATA DRILL

★ WHAT DOES BEING A LEADER MEAN TO ME?

★ IN WHAT WAYS CAN I BE A BETTER LEADER AT THE ACADEMY?

★ WHEN WAS THE LAST TIME I FAILED? WHAT DID I LEARN AND HOW CAN I APPLY THOSE LESSONS TO BEING A GOOD LEADER?

YEEESH. TOO LONG!
WILL ANSWER LATER.

★ WHAT SHOULD I DO WHEN I HAVE TO MAKE A DIFFICULT DECISION?

FACEHOOF.

KNOWING YOUR ROLE

A team member should know what role they play within the group structure. How does a cadet know what their role is? First, take stock of your strengths when interacting with your fellow cadets. What positive things do you take from group experiences? What do you enjoy about cooperation? What are accomplishments at which you excel? If you need help, consult with a group leader and have them evaluate your performance.

EXAMPLE

Starburst is keenly aware of her teammates' emotions. She/he knows when they're sad, frustrated, or feeling overwhelmed. Based on this information, we can assume that **Starburst** would excel in the role of a caretaker. As a caretaker, she/he would sensitively assess each team member's emotional state and offer them council based on her appraisal. She/he would then continue to communicate with her/his teammate after the fact in order to gauge the effectiveness of her/his advice.

DATA DRILL

★ WHAT ARE MY STRENGTHS?

★ WHAT ARE MY WEAKNESSES?

HAHA!

★ CAN I IDENTIFY THE ROLES OF MY
TEAMMATES?

★ HOW DO THE ACTIONS OF AN INDIVIDUAL
AFFECT THE GROUP?

LESSON #5

TEAMWORK

Working as a unit is beneficial to each and every team member. When a group of cadets work together, tasks can be completed quicker and more efficiently. What pony doesn't love *that*? TEAMWORK is about creating a support system of forward-thinking ponies who work in tandem to build better and more dynamic modes of thinking. There will be some team members who'll reject teamwork in favor of completing tasks on their own. This stubborn behavior is not uncommon among the pony community. That's why it's necessary to be patient. If you encounter a cadet who dismisses the help of their colleagues, be kind and explain to them the benefits of partnership. Teamwork can bring about great and positive change!

WONDERBOLTS

BLAZE

The Wonderbolts couldn't exist without teamwork. We'd fall apart! We're a ponyhood. We take care of one another. If I see one of my associates having a hard time, I always try to help out. That's just what a pony does. One time I saw Misty Fly struggling to do a loop-de-loop. She was having a lot of trouble, and I could tell it was making her upset. (She's cool with me telling this story.) I took her aside and showed her how to do it correctly. She was a little embarrassed, but that went away pretty quickly once she mastered the

technique. And in the end it worked out great because the team grew and got better. It's all about flying fast and lookin' good! Okay, maybe it's not all about that. I do like to fly fast, and I like to look good, though. I like other stuff, too, but you'll have to read my forthcoming autobiography, **BLAZE OF GLORY**, for the scoop on that. What is it about the Wonderbolts that keeps me around? I get to do what I love. Can't ask for more than that. *Blaze*

FLEETFOOT

Being in the Wonderbolts is awesome. We're all special in our own way, and I love that. When you're on a team of unique ponies, you get to hear a lot of different perspectives. Sometimes that can cause trouble. Ha-ha. (Don't ask Soarin about the time we got into a teensy little argument about who can do a better Sonic Rainboom.) And I get to travel and meet tons of cute stallions from all over Equestria. What? It's true. Stallions are fun to hang out with! But that's not why I do it. I do it because it keeps me disciplined and in control. The stuff I've learned from my fellow 'Bolts you can't learn anywhere else. And I get free stuff sometimes. What? Who doesn't love free stuff?!

Fleetfoot

MISTY FLY

I do it all for the fans!

Misty Fly

ACTIVITY

Each cadet must write down five positive aspects of working together as a team as well as five negative aspects of working at a team. When all the cadets in your group have completed this activity, read your responses aloud to the group and discuss what they mean. The goal of this activity is to share your hopes, fears, and any questions you might have. Listen to your fellow cadets and help those that are struggling to grasp the lesson.

REMEMBER:

Working as a team doesn't mean stifling the voice of your individual teammates. Cadets must be able to be themselves! Teamwork is not about surrendering your independent thought to a group

mind; it's about learning to find solutions that everypony can understand and from which they can benefit. Encourage your teammates to share their individual views and ideas. And if they're positive and support the group mission, use them. Teamwork, if applied correctly, empowers ponies to express their ideas in a safe and appreciative environment!

LESSON #6

COMMUNICATION

Communicate with your team. It's the best way to know what's happening with them. If you sense tension with a teammate, open up a dialogue about what might be troubling them. Talk it out! Sharing with the group fosters a sense of growth and safety that can be beneficial to a team in the long run. When team members hear shared thoughts and concerns voiced by colleagues, it makes them feel as if they're not alone. That's a very good thing! When team members are communicating, they are relating to one another and developing trust and cooperation. Make sure each team member knows their specific role. Delegate responsibility with efficiency and

understanding. Should a team member refuse their assigned role, listen to their concerns and explain to them why they were chosen. Describe the positive attributes they bring to the group that led to their selected position. If they continue to feel uncomfortable or unprepared, consider giving them a new station within the team. It's not worth it if a team member isn't happy.

Teamwork doesn't happen overnight. It takes time for a group to understand one another and come together. Observe your team members and how they interact. This helps foster growth.

DATA DRILL

★ AM I BETTER SHARING INFORMATION OR RECEIVING INFORMATION?

★ WHAT ARE SOME WAYS I CAN IMPROVE MY COMMUNICATION SKILLS?

Talk...more...clearly...er?

★ WHEN WAS THE LAST TIME I WAS FRUSTRATED BY BAD COMMUNICATION? WHAT WAS THE RESOLUTION?

UGH. These questions are stressing me out and I don't know how to express it and it feels like there's no end in sight!

ARE YOU HAPPY NOW, HANDBOOK?

LESSON #7

HANDLING CONFLICT

Listen up! This might be tough to hear. Working with others isn't always easy. Not everypony on a team will get along. But don't despair! This is called **CONFLICT**, and it often arises from the least-expected places at very inopportune times. That's why it's crucial to know how to resolve it calmly and respectfully. Should two cadets find themselves quarreling, take them aside and ask them to remain civil. There's never a need for name-calling! Ask them to listen to each other first and foremost, then put themselves in the other's hooves. Cadets should treat one another the way they would like to be treated. Encourage them to thoughtfully consider each other's position. Conflict doesn't always end easily, but a good team member inspires cadets who are in disagreement by targeting the deeper issues and speaking in a clear, thoughtful manner.

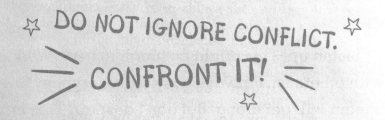

DO NOT IGNORE CONFLICT. CONFRONT IT!

DATA DRILL

LESSON #8

NEGATIVE ACTIONS

When a cadet behaves negatively, it can affect the group as a whole. Yikes! Nopony has time for that! Learn how to spot negative behavior and address it calmly and considerately so it doesn't put team morale and the ability to work together in jeopardy.

EXAMPLE

Stormfeather doesn't listen to his/her fellow team members when they share their thoughts and opinions. He/she rejects them outright. This makes them feel unheard and unappreciated. When it comes time to work together, Stormfeather's teammates do not feel comfortable working with him/her. They are afraid to speak their minds. This can cause secretive behaviors that color group interactions negatively. When this occurs over time, it sows the seeds for disloyalty, which can ultimately destroy a formerly high-functioning team situation.

DATA DRILL

★ WHAT ARE NEGATIVE ACTIONS?

Bad things

★ HOW CAN I SPOT THEM?

MY EYES

★ HAVE I EXHIBITED NEGATIVE ACTIONS?
(LIST SPECIFICS)   Sure

★ WHAT NEGATIVE ACTIONS HAVE I
OBSERVED IN OTHERS? WHAT CAN I DO
TO HELP CHANGE THEM?

Uh . . .

LESSON #9

TIPS

Nopony is perfect. Everypony makes mistakes! And those mistakes can be hard to see when *you're* the pony making them. A little advice can go a long way. TIPS are the offering of compassionate and practical solutions regarding your fellow teammates' work. It's about providing positive and hopeful comments regarding your teammates' performance with the intent to help them get better. It's important for a team to understand how and when to offer constructive criticism of their fellow teammates. In order to achieve a positive result, you may need to point out negative aspects of your teammates' performance so they can understand the root of the problem. Presenting negative comments isn't always easy and can be upsetting to hear.

TIPS FOR TRIUMPH

Provide feedback in a way that gives your teammate confidence, not doubt, that they can improve.

GOOD EXAMPLE

I NOTICED THAT SOMETHING YOU DID WAS SLIGHTLY OFF. I KNOW A GREAT WAY THAT YOU MIGHT BE ABLE TO CORRECT THAT ISSUE, AND I'D LOVE TO GIVE YOU SOME CONSTRUCTIVE CRITICISM THAT I THINK WILL HELP YOU ACHIEVE SUCCESS.

BAD EXAMPLE

YOU DID THAT ALL WRONG! YOU KEEP MESSING THINGS UP WHEN YOU NEED TO DO THEM CORRECTLY. WHAT'S YOUR PROBLEM? YOU LEARNED EVERYTHING JUST LIKE EVERYPONY ELSE. WHY CAN'T YOU JUST GET IT RIGHT?

DATA DRILL

- ✦ DO MY TEAMATES LOOK TO ME FOR FEEDBACK?

- ✦ WHAT ARE SOME OBSTACLES I HAVE IN SHARING IT?

- ✦ HOW DO I RECEIVE FEEDBACK?

- ✦ HAS THERE BEEN A TIME WHEN I WAS GIVEN NEGATIVE FEEDBACK AND HAD A HARD TIME ACCEPTING IT? WHAT WAS THE RESOLUTION?

TOOLONGTOOLONGTOOLONGTOOLONG
TOOLONGTOOLONGTOOLONGTOOLONG
TOOLONGTOOLONGTOOLONGTOOLONG.

LESSON #10

SUPPORTING YOUR TEAMMATES

Being on a team with many unique members can be challenging. But it's not impossible! That's why it's imperative to support your fellow team members when they need it. Sometimes it's easy to spot when your colleagues need help, and other times it can be tough to pin down. Keep your eyes peeled! Know when to rush in and lend an ear or a positive comment. Everypony needs an assist from time to time. Follow these steps in order to decide if your teammate needs a helping hand.

LISTEN

By listening to your teammate, you'll be able to gauge whether or not they're in need of some assistance. If they're struggling to understand something or complaining about the difficulty of an objective, use this as an "in" to ask them questions about the situation they're experiencing. How are they feeling? Are they expressing annoyance? Be mindful of their process, and use a positive tone when offering help.

LOOK

A teammate might not always verbalize their discomfort and frustration, so look for physical cues and emotional responses. How has your teammate's behavior changed? Has it become negative? Do they seem sad, angry, or embarrassed? Use the chart on the next page to help you out.

Happy   Sad   Angry   Excited

Afraid   Shy   Guilty   Tired

Jealous   Loved   Hopeful   Bored

Proud   Sorry   Embarrassed   Surprised

95

SITUATION:

Cadet #1 didn't quite complete a formation and gets visibly discouraged. After practice, Cadet #1 throws her uniform in a pile and stomps off sniffling.

RESPONSE:

Mention to Cadet #1 that you noticed what happened regarding the missed formation and let her know that even the best ponies make mistakes sometimes. Ask Cadet #1 if she'd like to talk about the situation and let her know you're available to chat anytime she needs to.

SIMPLE TIPS FOR TEAMMATES

Communicate! Check in with your teammates when you sense they might be having a tough time. Let them know you're there for them.

Don't brag! A team is comprised of many members, and they're all there because they're earned it. It's a group effort.

Stay involved! Make sure you play an active role in the growth of your team. When you have a good idea, share it. It might help take you to the next level.

Don't blame other cadets for your mistakes! Nopony likes to have a hoof pointed toward them in blame, especially when it's not their fault.

Be kind! Everypony has a tough time now and again. Be friendly and understanding when helping a teammate out.

TIPS FOR TRIUMPH

Be generous and patient with your teammates
when they seem to be struggling.

DATA DRILL

★ HOW CAN I BE THE BEST TEAMMATE I CAN BE?

★ HOW CAN I ENCOURAGE OTHER TEAMMATES TO BE BETTER?

★ WHAT ACTIVITIES CAN I DO WITH MY TEAMMATES TO MAKE US A STRONGER TEAM?

LESSON #11

TRAINING

The Wonderbolts Academy is a high-caliber training facility that offers a state-of-the-art aerial educational for cadets who are ready to rise above the competition. We strive to provide cadets with a positive and supportive atmosphere in which they're able to develop effective tools that aid in their growth. Training is essential to a cadet's physical and emotional development. Exertion is good for a cadet's well-being! Being active gets a cadet's juices flowing, and gives them more energy during the day. It also helps them clear their head by focusing on specific tasks. Practicing maneuvers is the best way to perfect them. Nopony learns how to complete a Sonic Rainboom just by reading about it in a book. It takes hard work and a bunch of sweat to be able to fly in the big leagues. Completing the Wonderbolts exercise regimen is a pivotal part of the training process. Some cadets will rise, and some ponies will fall. Which will you do?

PONY SEE AND PONY DO! MOVE THOSE HAUNCHES TILL THEY'RE BLUE!

WING LIFTS

A pony has to build strength! Wing lifts can boost a cadet's wing power quite considerably, allowing them more control during flight. Begin with twenty repetitions and increase as needed.

BARREL ROLLS

A barrel roll is when a cadet makes a complete rotation in flight. The trick is to do it while maintaining speed and direction.

OBSTACLE COURSE

The Wonderbolts obstacle course features a series of physical feats through which a cadet must navigate in order to succeed. This challenge helps develop a cadet's agility and aerial navigation skills.

FLAG DRILL

Cadets are divided into two teams. Each team is assigned a colored flag, which they are tasked to retrieve. The team that finds the most of the flags of the opposing team's color wins. For added difficulty, set a clock and give both teams a limited time frame to collect the flags!

DIZZITRON

The Dizzitron is a highly advanced, revolutionary device that spins a cadet around in circles until they're very dizzy. Their objective is to then fly as straight as they can and land safely on the tarmac. This teaches a cadet precision and recovery.

105

✦ FORMATIONS & MANEUVERS ✦

The Wonderbolts are known for their dazzling and sophisticated aerial formations. Many of these movements were choreographed by the famous Wonderbolt Commander Easyglider. While some configurations have changed over time, Easyglider's effortless sky dances remain relatively unchanged and continue to mesmerize audiences to this day.

CHEVRON FORMATION

The Chevron formation is a symmetrical V-shaped flight pattern. The purpose of this formation is for cadets to learn how to stay together and follow the lead pony, who is located at the tip of the V.

ICARANIAN SUN SALUTATION

Princess Celestia's favorite Wonderbolts formation is the Icaranian Sun Salutation.

HOT TIP: Dihedral wing angles can help increase stability in banking turns.

MY JAM!

SONIC RAINBOOM

The most famous and memorable Wonderbolts maneuver is the dazzling Sonic Rainboom. When a pony reaches top speed, a loud boom is created that sends out a brightly colored rainbow shockwave in all directions. Educationally speaking, the maneuver is meant to convey the raw power of a pony's speed. Visually speaking, it's a real crowd pleaser.

AW YEAH!

I am so great at personal fan art!

WONDERBOLTS
✦ OF THE FUTURE ✦
CLOUDSDALE FLIGHT CAMP

Ponies who are a bit too young for the
Wonderbolts Academy are welcome to attend
Cloudsdale's premier Flight Camp. Here they'll
learn the basics of flight. Who knows? Their idols,
the Wonderbolts, might stop by for a visit.

Scootaloo
would love this!

DATA DRILL

★ **WHAT IS MY FAVORITE ASPECT OF TRAINING?**

NOT ANSWERING THESE QUESTIONS!

★ **WHAT DO I NEED TO IMPROVE ON?**

★ **WHAT IS MY FAVORITE FORMATION TO COMPLETE AND WHY?**

When you need a Sonic Rainboom, you call Rainbow Dash. Why?

Because I rule the sky.

Hey, that rhymes!

COMPETITION & CONDUCT

Competition is a valuable tool that helps unlock a cadet's true potential! It's not about winning; it's about developing your skills in an ambitious environment. During competition, a cadet is able to assess their level of skill against other trained rivals. This will show them what areas may need improvement. Don't get discouraged if you find yourself coming up a little short. Stay positive and make a plan to increase your studies in order to meet your goals. Competition isn't about showing off or belittling your opponents; it's about rising to the occasion and finding out what kind of pony you are when the heat is on.

A cadet's conduct must always be exemplary during competition. Some ponies like to be hurtful to their competitors before a big race in order to throw them off and distract them from winning. This is unacceptable behavior. Cadets must always support one another, even in competition. Disrespecting your competitors is discouraged and considered poor sportsponyship. Always treat rivals with respect, no matter the situation.

BEST YOUNG FLYER CONTEST

The Best Young Flyer Contest is a chance for young ponies to get a taste of competition on a basic level as they race across the sky, entertaining the crowds.

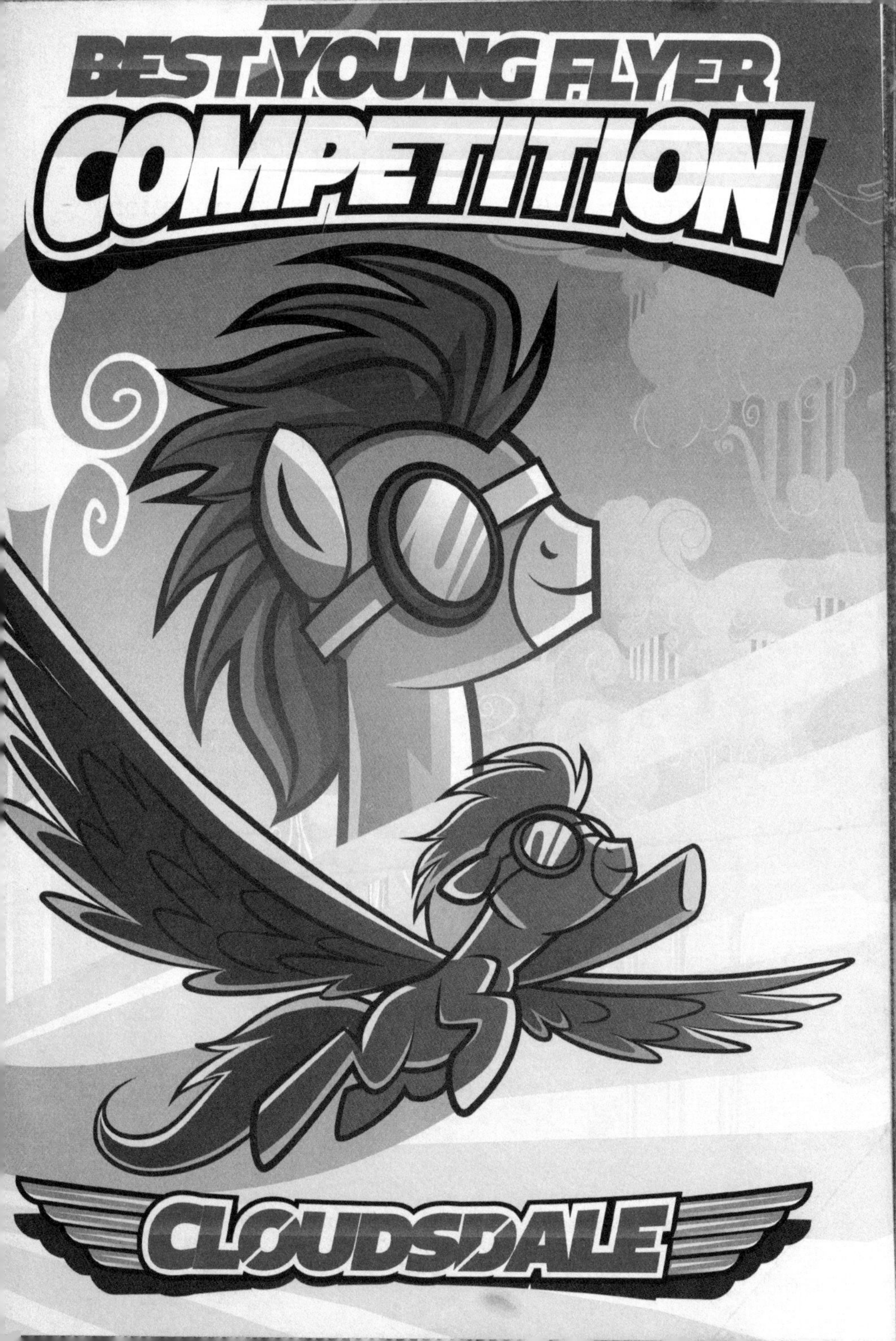
BEST YOUNG FLYER
COMPETITION
CLOUDSDALE

LUCY PACKARD, PONY PREPPER

"I am *living* for the Best Young Flyer competition. These young ponies out here are just incredible. Such an inspiration. It's my job to get them ready for competition and keep them in line backstage. It's not easy! There are a lot of them. Sometimes there's too much chitter-chatter and not enough preparation. But I will say this: There's also style, professionalism, and technique. You don't get to be a Wonderbolt without those things, trust me."

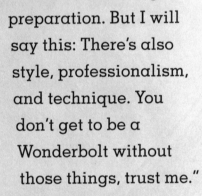

MADDEN, ANNOUNCER

"I've seen a lot of Best Young Flyers in my day but they never cease to amaze me. Such talent and energy. It means a lot for these ponies to be able to show off their stuff, I'll tell you that. It means even more when they do. Cloudsdale is a wonderful place to learn how to make that happen."

CLOUDSDALE CHEERLEADER #1

"We love cheering at competitions! But we don't compete with one another, though. Not really. Well, maybe. Sometimes. **Go, Cloudsdale!**"

SPRING STEP, CLOUDSDALE CHEERLEADER

"I just designed the uniforms!"

WONDERBOLTS DERBY

One of the highlights of being a Wonderbolt is participating in the exciting Wonderbolts Derby. Only the most exemplary ponies are chosen to fly in this kingdom-renowned competition for the ages. Notable names and celebrities from across Equestria wear their finest fashions as they gather to celebrate excellence in flight.

FANCY PANTS

"I just love the Wonderbolts Derby! They go so fast. It's very exciting. I'll be honest, though: I come for the hats and fashions more than anything. It's all about rubbing hooves with the highest of society and looking fabulous while doing it. Go, Wonderbolts!"

TIPS FOR TRIUMPH

Remember that competitions are not just tests of physical skill, but of sportsponyship.

GOOD EXAMPLE

BAD EXAMPLE

DATA DRILL

⭐ WHY IS COMPETITION IMPORTANT?

⭐ HOW IMPORTANT IS COMPETITION IN COMPARISON TO OTHER ASPECTS OF MY TRAINING?

⭐ IS IT MORE IMPORTANT TO WIN OR TO LOSE?

✫ Winning > all things! ✫

LESSON #13

STAYING TRUE TO YOURSELF

Being unique and staying true to yourself is a big part of the Wonderbolts lifestyle. While teamwork is both necessary and encouraged, it doesn't mean that you should be like every other cadet. Sometimes it's hard to know how to be yourself, especially when you're still finding out who that is! Here are some trust **DOs** and **DON'Ts** that will help you in your journey.

★ **DO** embrace who you are and work to understand yourself on a deeper level.

★ **DON'T** put pressure on yourself to be like other ponies.

★ **DO** respect others' uniqueness and treat them as you'd want to be treated.

★ **DON'T** disrespect ponies because they're different than you.

★ **DO** spend time by yourself and use it to reflect on who you want to be.

★ **DON'T** spend so much time with others that you become exactly like them.

★ **DO** experiment with style. It's okay to shake things up once in a while for fun!

- ⭐ **DON'T** wear the same thing all the time. Chances are you'll get bored.

- ⭐ **DO** stand up for yourself.

- ⭐ **DON'T** let other ponies push you to be somepony you're not.

- ⭐ **DO** take your time and get to know yourself. No need to rush.

- ⭐ **DON'T** force yourself to be somepony you're not.

- ⭐ **DO** try different things. That's how you find out what you really like.

- ⭐ **DON'T** always do the same things.

- ⭐ **DO** be as authentic and real as you can be.

- ★ **DON'T** act fake and phony.

- ★ **DO** listen to other pony's unique perspectives.

- ★ **DON'T** shut your peers out of discussions.

- ★ **DO** stay confident and calm when things get hectic. You've got this!

- ★ **DON'T** lose control when you feel over-whelmed. It gets better.

- ★ **DO** help ponies who are struggling to figure out who they are.

- ★ **DON'T** reject ponies because they are different.

- ★ **DO** spend time with ponies who inspire and support you.

★ **DON'T** spend time with negative ponies with bad attitudes.

★ **DO** understand that you face challenges and seek counsel from friends when you need it.

★ **DON'T** pretend everything is fine when you are feeling down. Ask for help.

★ **DO** learn to be comfortable in your own skin. It's the only skin you've got.

★ **DON'T** worry about what others think of how you look. It's not worth your time.

★ **DO** consider the good advice of the pony peers who care about you.

★ **DON'T** be too concerned with what other ponies think. Stay on *your* path.

- ★ **DO** think critically about the issues that mean the most to you.

- ★ **DON'T** adopt a certain perspective to impress another pony.

- ★ **DO** have a sense of humor! It's always okay to laugh at yourself.

- ★ **DON'T** get wound too tight. Everything will be okay.

REMEMBER: The only pony out there
who is like **YOU** is **YOU!**

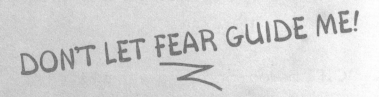

DON'T LET FEAR GUIDE ME!

FLAIRE d'MARE
★ TELLS IT LIKE IT IS ★

Legendary fashion icon Flaire d'Mare did it all. She designed clothing for everypony from Celestia to Admiral Fairy Flight, and even ran her own boutique, **Beware the FLAIR.** Ever since she was a small foal, she knew she was different. She loved boldness and color. Growing up in a small community like San Palomino, Flaire d'Mare didn't always have the opportunity to be herself. She liked dressing in outrageous clothes and causing quite a stir. Her family loved her dearly, but they didn't always understand her unique

Rarity's idol!

style. Flaire d'Mare always dreamed of moving to a big, bustling city, and when she was old enough, that was exactly what she did! She studied at the Equestria Institute for Fashion, where she was able to put her passion for style to good use. After studying hard, honing her skills, and graduating with excellent grades, she moved to Cloudsdale, where she got her very first job—dressing the Wonderbolts! It was her job to reimagine the Wonderbolts' iconic uniform for a

new generation, and she jumped at the chance. She's become one of Equestria's most famous and exclusive designers. Here is an exerpt of a famous interview she did with *PRANCE* magazine.

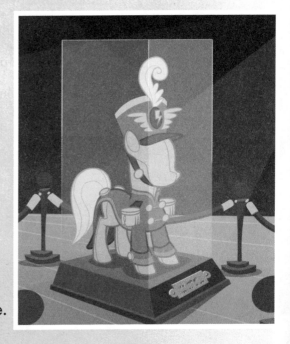

PRANCE

Some might say that the original Wonderbolts uniforms were unattractive, and I can certainly understand that. They didn't *say* anything. They had no *pizazz*. The fabrics couldn't breathe and were much too itchy for movement. How could those ponies *stand* it? Equestria has changed since those simpler times, and my newest designs reflect that. They're streamlined and modern. They say, 'I'm a pony of the sky, and I'm not afraid to be bold!' Ponies perspire when they're doing all those loops and twirls, but the audience will never see them sweat. I made that happen. Of course, not every one of my designs was a hit. We experimented with a lot of looks through the centuries. Life is about *trying different things*! A fashion designer is bound to make a slight mistake every so often."

PRANCE

The Wonderbolts logo is recognized across Cloudsdale and all of Equestria as a symbol of service and spirit. When ponies see the Winged Bolt, they're inspired by their high-flying heroes to always do their best. But things might have been different had they chosen a different insignia.

"The logo is simple, and I like that. The Wonderbolts put all the drama into their exciting aerial routine, not in their attire. You just can't improve upon perfection!"
— FLAIRE d'MARE

ACTIVITY: START A VISION BOARD

A cadet must always stay inspired! Why not start a vision board with unique things that inspire you to be the best pony you can be?

My friends!

LESSON #14

SUPPORT NETWORK

Being a Wonderbolt is a full-time job. Ponies have to commit themselves to training full time and being available for anything that comes their way. So when something comes up that takes a team member out of the sky, an eager young Wonderbolt Reservist is pulled up from the ranks to take that pony's coveted place. While reservists wait for their turn among the clouds, they stay focused by training hard. That way they can be ready when the time comes for them to ascend the ladder of responsibility. A reservist is always prepared to support a fellow Wonderbolt should they need it!

The Wonderbolt Reservists are part of what is known as a **SUPPORT NETWORK**. This is a system of friends and colleagues that a pony can count on for advice when things get tough. A strong support network is crucial to maintaining balance and can also include family members, teachers, and ponies you trust. Keep in touch with them and let them know how you're doing. Other ponies don't always know what you're going through, so if you need a little help along the way, don't be afraid to ask for it.

Going from a young cadet to a Wonderbolt Reservist is a big step. Many eager cadets are anxious to make it to the big leagues, but you shouldn't forget that everything is a learning process. Be patient and continue your studies. Everypony's time will come sooner or later.

SUNSHOWER RAINDROPS: "We're **WINGPONIES**, which means that we have one another's hindquarters no matter what. We look after one another, and make sure we're safe and stuff like that. Maybe one day we'll get to be full-fledged Wonderbolts. Hooves crossed!"

THUNDERLANE: "YEAH! What she said!"

FLARE d'MAIRE: "The Wonderbolts Reservists are a wonderful group of ponies and I wanted their uniforms to reflect that. They're quite special in that respect. I think it's a wonderful thing to be able to be there for your fellow ponies. Some reservists may have to wait their entire lives to become Wonderbolts, but they still show up to support. What patience! I certainly couldn't do it. Regardless, they need to look good. Their uniforms are a bit more casual, because they're not quite there yet. But they will be one day! Hopefully."

DATA DRILL

★ ARE RESERVISTS LESS IMPORTANT THAN WONDERBOLTS?

★ WHY ARE RESERVISTS IMPORTANT?

★ DO I WANT TO BE A RESERVIST?

STUDY GUIDE

What are three ways to promote teamwork?

_____

List three ways to support your teammates.

_____

What is respect?

_____

Do you know what your role is? Describe it in detail.

MY ROLL IS BUTTERED! _____

What are three ways to handle conflict?

Walk away? _____

HISTORY POP QUIZ

Name: Rainbow Dash

88%

Nice work, Cadet!

What do the initials E.U.P. stand for?

Equestria United Ponies

For whom did the original aerial team perform?

EVERYPONY!

Okay, but looking for those in attendance at the celebration for Equestria's first Celestial Year of Peace

The Wonderbolts were given their name by which famous Pegasus?

General Firefly

What is the name of the premiere Wonderbolts choreographer?

Commander Easyglider

How many Pegasi flew in the original Wonderbolts squad?

Seven

What is the Wonderbolts motto?

Soaring Higher   Utentes Superiores

Do you know Princess Celestia's favorite flight pattern?

Icranian Sun
Salutation

Who led the Wonderbolts in the Fourth Celestial Era?
Col. Purple Dart

CADET JOURNAL

RAINBOW DASH'S
VERY PRIVATE
AND PERSONAL
JOURNAL OF
WONDERBOLT LIFE

Wonderbolt Academy Trials!!!!!

07:20 TEAM BRIEFING!!! (because there were 20 ponies in the original EUP honor guard)

TRIALS

Things to keep an eye out for: sloppy wing placement, crooked lines, basic technique, form, attention to detail

I heard a rumor that some ponies fly **SO MUCH** during their trials that their wings fall off. **HOW DO I MAKE THAT NOT HAPPEN?**

Each pony will be judged on speed, strength, agility, and technique. Then they'll have a **FINAL EVALUATION.**

Should I make preflight checklists?????
REMEMBER TO CLEAN UNIFORM!!!
What is **GUSTO?** Somepony told me I needed more of this.

STUFF EVERY
WONDERBOLT NEEDS

Wing Balm
a mirror
attitude
grace
sunglasses
a style mentor
catchphrase
nickname
THE PERFECT SADDLE BAG

LIST OF POSSIBLE NICKNAMES

Dashinator

MISS DASH 'Bow

Care
Mare

Captain
Awesome

Dynamic Dash

Reading Rainboom

Rainbow FLASH

The Dash

Rainbow
SMASH

Forthright Filly

GOALS

⚡ Beat Wind Rider's record for fastest long-distance flight

⚡ What is WING SYMMETRY?

⚡ Come up with flight patterns and stuff

⚡ Gain confidence!

DAY ONE

Today was my first day at the Wonderbolt Academy, and it was SO AMAZING. Last night? Not so much. I was really nervous. My stomach was in knots. I know that sounds really amateurish, but it's not. A lot of famous ponies get nervous before, you know, big events. It means they're thinking about it too much or something. OH!!! I had a WEIRD dream, too. It didn't make any sense! Do you want to hear it? Okay, I'll tell you. In my dream I was flying all over Equestria, looking for Rarity's favorite dress (?). THEN I lost my cutie mark and Nightmare Moon told me I had to go eat one of Applejack's pies to get strength so I could win the Best Young Flyer Competition, but then I was running late so I put on my mystery mask (?) and took off. I got to the Competition, and it was already OVER! I'd missed the whole thing. Spike was there, so he gave me a hug because I was upset. AND THEN I WOKE UP. I don't know what any of it

means, but I bet it has to do with my feeling nervous.
YIKES! I got way off track. Anyway, back to my first
day. It was AMAZING. I already said that, but it's true.
Spitfire was pretty tough on everypony, including me.
Not in a mean way, but in a way that helps us see our
mistakes and learn from them. Uh-oh. Lights-out in
the Barracks. GAH! I'll write more later. Maybe.
Gotta go!

DAY FOUR

Sorry I didn't write anything
on Day 2 and Day 3, but I've been
REALLY busy with everything. It's A LOT of work. I've
been thinking about something, too. Before I got
here, I thought every day would be a dream come true.
I'd get up in the morning, go for a quick flight around
campus, and then settle into my day of studies and
training. Oh no, ponygirl! I WISH it were that easy.
We have to get up SO EARLY and there's no time to

do the stuff we want because we're on such a tight schedule. Fast Clip is one of my supervisors, and he doesn't let us do ANYTHING that's not on his agenda. I had to go to the bathroom REALLY BAD yesterday five minutes before our scheduled break time and when I asked him if I could go a little bit early, he said, "There's a reason we do things the way we do them here at the Wonderbolts Academy."

I said, "Is that a NO, sir?" and he just STARED AT ME. I almost wet myself. But I didn't.

What else? I was in a group with Bulk Biceps today, which was interesting. The other cadets are pretty cool. I'm meeting a lot of new ponies and making new friends as much as possible. That's one of the best parts about being here. We're like a family that's just getting to know one another! Bulk Biceps is kind of like a cousin that ponies love even though he's a little weird. Well, I'm tired now. G'NIGHT!

DAY EIGHT

I'M SO BEHIND ON MY JOURNAL! The way I see it is that I came here to **EXPERIENCE** things, not write down everything I did. Also, I'm exhausted every single night, so I don't always feel like doing anything. I took my first quiz today. When Whiplash was handing them out he looked right at me in a very weird way. I think he knew that I wasn't prepared. I mean, I **STUDIED, OF COURSE**, but there's so much information to memorize. I don't think my brain can remember it all. I also have a flying test coming up. That should be easy. It's basic stuff like

Sonic Rainbooms, which I know everything about. I hope I don't get nervous and mess it up. **GAH!** Why did I just write that? Now I'm jinxed! Wait a minute. I don't believe in jinxes. Okay, clearly, I've been up too long and I'm losing my mind. I'm going to go to bed now.

DAY NINE

It's the second day in a row that I'm writing in my journal! Pat on the back, Dash-i-nator. (I'm experimenting with nicknames.) Today is our free day to do anything we want, so most of the ponies are sleeping in, but I woke up early so I could write. Also, I didn't sleep that well. I think I miss my friends. I know, I know. I'm living my dream! But I wouldn't be here without the support and love of my friends. They're the ones who helped me believe in myself enough to make it this far. I have to keep going. Ugh, that sounds so serious! It's not THAT serious. Nopony ever said it was going to be easy, but I wish it didn't have to be SO HARD. Thankfully, it's a FUN hard. My tummy is grumbling, so I'm going to go eat something. Some of the other cadets said they're going into Cloudsdale later to shop and see some of the sights. I haven't decided if I'm going to join them. Sorry I haven't been writing in you a lot, Journal. I have been writing letters to my friends back in Ponyville. You understand, I'm sure. You're a good journal.

DAY TWELVE

Today was **VERY COOL**, and we didn't even fly! All the cadets sat in a circle and talked about what being at the Wonderbolts Academy meant to us. Everypony shared a personal story. It's what Applejack would call "touchy-feely" stuff. Some ponies did **NOT** want to talk about personal stuff. One pony (who shall remain nameless) said her family told her that becoming a Wonderbolt was the **ONLY** thing in the world, and that if she didn't do it, they would be very disappointed in her. I don't think that's fair at all! Ponies should get to follow their own dreams. Pushing somepony into doing something they don't want to do is **DANGEROUS**. Then that pony feels trapped, and feeling trapped is the worst feeling in the whole world. I told the pony (who shall remain nameless) that she should calmly and politely tell her family that she wants to choose her own path. I also offered to go with her when she tells them in case she needs support. Even if she doesn't want to be a Wonderbolt, she'll always have a friend in me. I don't know if I'll write in this journal again because I'm running out of space (they should put more pages in here!), but I'm having the time of my life. That's all there is to say about that!

DAY ??????

I'm stressed. What if I don't make it on the Wonderbolts?!?! What if I only make to the Reserves?! SIGH. What am I saying? I'm not even a graduate of the Academy yet, but one day I will be, and even if I don't get on the team the first time, there's always the next time. Who knows? Maybe I'll make the Reserves! If anything happens to one of the Wonderbolts, I'll be ready and waiting to swoop in and take their place (honorably of course). Oh well, back to dreaming....

APPLICATION & ESSAY

NAME: *Rainbow Dash*

USE THREE POSITIVE WORDS TO DESCRIBE YOURSELF:

Loyal, Passionate, Competitive

WHAT DO YOU HOPE TO LEARN AT THE WONDERBOLTS ACADEMY?

I hope to learn how to be an inspiration to all the ponies in Equstria and teach them that if you study hard and follow your passion, you can have success. I also want to learn how to fly really, really fast.

WHAT IS A VALUABLE LESSON YOU HAVE LEARNED?

I believe it's very important to help ponies who are in need, and I try to help whenever I can. In one instance, I helped so many ponies that they heaped a lot of praise on me. It felt very good, but it made me too prideful. I got a big head and lost sight of the reason I was helping ponies in the first place. In the end, I learned that doing good deeds is its own reward.

WHERE DID YOU HEAR ABOUT THE WONDERBOLTS ACADEMY?

 Flyer

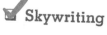 Friend

☑ Skywriting

 A Dream

❏ Cereal Box

❏ Singing Telegram

❏ Other

WHY DO YOU WANT TO ATTEND THE WONDERBOLTS ACADEMY?

The first time I saw the Wonderbolts, I knew I had to be one. They're not only the premiere aerialists of our time but an inspiration to ponies of all ages. Their dedication to their abilities is impressive and commendable. Over the years, many things happened to me that led me to believe it's my destiny to become a full-fledged member of the Wonderbolts team. A while ago, a group of weird dark Pegasi called the Shadowbolts tried to lure me away from a very important mission. They were actually Nightmare Moon in disguise. It's a long story. Anyway, they thought that I wanted to be a Wonderbolt so badly that I'd believe anything they said. They thought they'd be able to trick me into abandoning my friends, but that didn't happen. I resisted their bait and ended up gaining the Element of Loyalty for my efforts. It made me realize that training and commitment were the next step in my journey.

Then I became obsessed with Sonic Rainbooms. I've always thought they were very entertaining but completing one in front of a crowd was somewhat frightening. I worried about failing and put a lot of pressure on myself to succeed. My friends believe in me very much. What if I let them down? I was ultimately able to focus and complete my task with success.

I have dealt with many things that have frustrated and upset me, including bullying and insecurity about my small wings. Thankfully, my friends have always been there to support me. They inspire me to not only follow my dreams but be a better pony. I look at the Wonderbolts, and I see an opportunity to be a role model and share a positive message that nopony is alone and, together, we're all able to achieve great things. When I see the Wonderbolts soar majestically through the clouds, it's not only very cool, but it makes me remember I'm not alone. I believe if I am selected to become a student at the Wonderbolts Academy, I will not only excel in my studies, but I will also graduate to full Wonderbolts membership and become a guiding spirit to the ponies of the future.

I am so proud of you! This admissions committee will LOVE this essay! -Twilight

THE OFFICIAL
WONDERBOLTS
CATALOG

A MALL IN THE SKY!

COMING SOON
WONDERBOLTS
THE MOVIE
In a land where the sky's the limit, these ponies soar above the clouds.
THIS ISN'T A FLYBY!

* *
You're going to do
* GREAT!!!!!
* * WE LOVE YOU!!
* Pinkie Pie *
* * *

WONDERBOLTS PONYHOOD OF THE SKY

SPITFIRE

FLEET FOOT

WAVE CHILL

BLAZE

MISTY FLY

SILVER LINING

SURPRISE

FIRE STREAK

SOARIN

LIGHTNING STREAK

LIGHTNING DASH

HIGH WINDS

WONDERBOLT CADETS FUTURE FLIERS

RAINBOW DASH

That's me!

MIDNIGHT STRIKE

SUNSHOWER RAINDROPS

PARASOL

ORANGE SWIRL

CLOUD CHASER

WILD FIRE

PIZZELLE

STORMFEATHER

**SPRINKLE
MEDLEY**

STARBURST

STARRY EYES

WONDERBOLT CADETS FUTURE FLIERS

STAR HUNTER

BULK BICEPS

CLOUD KICKER

WARM FRONT **RAINBOW SWOOP** **CRESCENT PONY**